An ex-newspaperman now in his seventies, Harrison started writing some fifteen years ago while living in a remote, mountainous area of Spain.

Just A Tick

Harrison Gee

Just A Tick

Vanguard Press

VANGUARD PAPERBACK

© Copyright 2011
Harrison Gee

The right of Harrison Gee to be identified as author of
this work has been asserted by him in accordance with the
Copyright, Designs and Patents Act 1988.

A CIP catalogue record for this title is
available from the British Library.

ISBN 978 1 43868767

*Vanguard Press is an imprint of
Pegasus Elliot MacKenzie Publishers Ltd.*
www.pegasuspublishers.com

First Published in 2011

**Vanguard Press
Sheraton House Castle Park
Cambridge England**

Printed & Bound in Great Britain

For Doreen with love

"Night night, darling"

CONTENTS

I
OUTSIDE HELP

"Can I speak to Doreen please?" It was a simple enough request. It was while I was putting the final touches to a long overdue painting chore in the small bedroom that the phone had rung, announcing a rare call. Gratefully deserting the irksome task, I hurried to answer the electronic summons, en route wiping away from my fingers the clinging result of an earlier, careless overloading of the complaining paintbrush.

That the question threw me, would surprise no one aware of the fact that Doreen had passed away some six years earlier. The enquiry was perhaps even more surprising since her illness had been prolonged and, as far as I was aware, all close friends and family were conscious of the tragic situation. Indeed, as now I struggled to find an answer to who this might be, I realised that involuntarily the breath was all but gone from my body.

Then it struck me. 'Could this be a mistake?'

"Sorry, but are you sure you have the right number?" – the only rational response coming to mind somehow finding its way to my lips.

"Well, I think so," came the now perhaps not so certain reply. "That is 707 555437 isn't it?"

Now I was really flummoxed. Whoever the lady was, certainly she had dialled correctly.

Automatically I asked: "Who is it calling, please?" A sensitive explanation was needed and before choosing the right words, it was necessary to know the caller's previous relationship with my wife.

Now I sensed a degree of impatience in the voice, the answer given serving only to exacerbate the situation. "Well look," said the voice, more than a little tinged with the brogue of England's north-east, "I doubt she'd remember me by name but, we met at the library in town a week or so ago. You might say 'purely a passing acquaintance'. Standing alongside one another, searching the fiction shelves, we reached simultaneously for the same title. With only a single copy available, recognising the awkwardness of the situation, with embarrassed smiles, politely we both held back, each allowing the other first handling.

"Doreen, however, kindly conceded, insisting that I borrow it first. In that I promised to let her know when I had finished with it, hence the exchange of telephone numbers and this call."

Where to go from here? Quite obviously this was a mistake. "Look," I began, not really knowing what to say, nevertheless voicing my only thoughts, "despite you having the right name and the right number, I'm afraid that either some sort of mistake has been made or, if you'll forgive me, this must be a practical joke – although, I must say, it would be in very poor taste. You see, the only Doreen at this address was my former wife who, unfortunately passed away some time ago. So as you will understand, the lady you refer to could not possibly be her."

Indignation now played its part in the awkward proceedings. "Well look," proclaimed the voice, the brogue intensifying, "this is certainly no practical joke." Then realising her own part in the matter, the still unnamed female added: "I'm sorry if my call has upset you, but I can assure you that all I am doing is fulfilling a promise I made to the lady. But given the truth in what you tell me, I have to agree that something here seems very wrong. Like you, no doubt, I find the whole matter perplexing; especially as we got to know one another rather better than I have so far explained. In fact following our meeting, Doreen and I went for a coffee together – though, truth be known, she preferred tea."

Those last few words went home. Hadn't it always been the way? Doreen, was seriously addicted to tea. And coffee, certainly would not have been on Doreen's agenda. Nevertheless, none of this was making sense. It was impossible; although the sincerity registered in the voice could not be questioned.

"Well, I'm lost for any other sort of explanation," I told her bluntly, expressing exactly my feelings in the matter. However, tempering its effect, sensitively I added: "Though I must say I don't doubt your honesty and neighbourly motive."

Time was passing and the caller, making no move to back away from the situation, suggested she might be willing to help find a rational explanation. "Look," I said, pursuing the thought, "you may think this is somewhat of an imposition, but if, like me, you are interested in solving this mystery, I wonder if sometime in the near future, you would care to meet? Not that I, in any way, believe in an afterlife, but perhaps a photo of my wife would help to clear that possibility out of the way. What do you say?" The rest was a formality and a meeting arranged in town, at the same small cafe near to the library the following day.

"It was all so real, even the meeting itself." Strangely, telling Ruji somehow relieved the stress in me; although, characteristically she dismissed it all for what it was, simply a dream. Whatever her reaction, I suppose revealing to my now wife those things that were uppermost in my obviously troubled mind, had the effect of releasing the growing pressure of mental stress.

Doreen, of course, and her death, still held fast in my memory. Then there was the book. Its writing had occupied me fully, all in all for some eleven months. No wonder the two events had together manifested themselves in mental images during sleep-time. Perhaps it was nature's way of offering to my inner self a degree of relief from the worry.

"What was most disturbing," I further recounted the train of dreamed events to Ruji, "from Doreen's photograph, my now new female friend recognised her likeness immediately. The whole thing was weird. A totally inexplicable experience." And that is how it all began, this journey through, what might be described by others as, make-believe, all imagination.

But, strictly speaking, that could not be held to be true. For as anyone witness to my efforts in the writing of an earlier book will confirm my claim was, that in so doing, never once, so it seemed, had I been totally alone, many times the words seeming not to be mine – they being whispered at my ear by an unknown force or being.

But now, here was an influence even stronger, disconcertingly one affecting conscious behaviour. For, whenever out and about I would find myself searching faces, illogically intent on finding Doreen. It was as though she was lost and sadly her only hope of reaching home was my finding her. In retrospect I suppose it was the behaviour of a soul close to the point of madness. But for that to happen, there is a need for witnesses. However, recognising it for what it was, other than the substance of my dream, nothing further was imparted to Ruji.

As time passed the search grew less intense, although occasionally a glimpse of someone of similar looks and stature often would revive the nonsensical habit. Then, a few weeks on, I encountered a dream sequel. Again whilst at my decorating chore, the lady of previous meeting again telephoned. This time it was to enquire whether I had solved the mystery.

Unlike all previous dreams in memory, on this occasion having awoken with it in mind, I must have had the presence of mind to ask the lady's name and, relating to her original phone-call, the title of the book concerned. Her name, Tollie Bembridge, raised no memory from the depths. The title of the book, however, *But A Fleeting Shadow* by Harrison Gee, did. Written under a pen name, it was none but mine own, surprising me greatly. Perhaps more so since at that time it was yet to be published.

And so real time passed with, in nights of fitful sleep, no repeat performance. By day, out of the house the search for Doreen was sometimes resumed. At home, from those listed in The Writer's Handbook, the hunt for a willing literary agent or publisher for my book continued.

Polite they may have been but, refusals came, so it seemed as if little more than a glance had been afforded to the synopsis. Perhaps not surprising since, apparently, learned from some of the apologetic replies, such manuscripts are produced at a prodigious rate, some agents receiving over two hundred per week. As a nation famously noted for being shopkeepers, seemingly hours of business are limited, since today the national pastime appears to have changed to the writing of books.

But as the search continued in the writer's bible for an appropriate publishing agent, came the shock of my life. For there sandwiched between the lines of type, as it seemed to me boldly highlighted, was the name 'Tollie Bembridge'.

My physical being was as though scorched by a searing bolt from the blue. It seemed senses were deceiving me. But, after blinking hard to clear my sight, a fresh look confirmed the impossible. The name was that of the lady in my dreams.

Also gleaned from the text, yet another surprising fact was, that this particular agent, if only coincidence, had represented Doreen's favourite writer, 'Katie Goodson', the renowned, North Eastern authoress, herself now sadly passed on.

It took me all of 24 hours to pluck up the courage to lift the phone and dial the London number. Previously, approaches had been made by post. Negatively perhaps, though no doubt realistically, I surmised that agents rather than be plagued continuously by would-be authors over the phone, preferred it that way. This time however, something pressured me into changing the manner of approach.

Surprisingly, the voice on the other end of the line was more welcoming than expected. But, having asked to speak to my erstwhile acquaintance, I was dealt the greatest shock of all. Tragically, only a few weeks earlier Tollie Bembridge had been killed in a road accident.

"Hello! Hello! Are you still there caller?" was all I heard – hearing being the only sense still unimpaired. Struggling through a fog of befuddlement, with wits lost somewhere between reality and mysticism, voice was recovered and registered its presence with a stammered: "Yes, yes, I'm still here."

"I can put you through to Mrs Bembridge's replacement if you like," – the helpful proposition from the receptionist.

That after all previous disappointments my work was eventually accepted, may be surprising. It certainly was to me.

Indeed, how the gods or whatever powers were working on my behalf managed this minor miracle, certainly defies rational explanation. For my own part, I like to believe that somehow Doreen was once more taking care of her own. And if any one dear soul knew how to do that, it was my darling Doreen.

Oh, and the paint job in the small bedroom? Well, perhaps I should have put more thought into starting the job on my own. Another example maybe, of the need to consider bringing in outside help?

II
YOUNG AT HEART

For someone to be born to parents of the surname Younger, never struck me as anything unusual, until, that is, I reached my early sixties. Until then, unlike many of my peers, the inevitable march of time, as most markedly recorded as one passes from one tenth of a century to another, seemed to have had, if any, little psychological effect on me.

But lately, now traversing the years of my sixties and suddenly, as I am, faced with the realism of perhaps not too many years of life in reserve, increasingly I am aware of the demise of those around me; particularly those of my own generation and of course those older. Time, or rather its passing, has suddenly become, for me, more noticed.

Then again, life amongst the living isn't always a sparkling affair, with, amongst many friends, conversations depressingly centred on methods of prolonging life and within this, not least, the minimising of the body's level of cholesterol – at this time, over-eaten decidedly recognised as a killer.

Until now, the reader will have discovered that, grammatically, this account of happenings, despite being of the past, has been offered in the present tense. What follows, hopefully may explain this incongruity.

For it was following one of my recent, regular evening visits to the local hostelry for a few relaxing beers, that in later setting off for home I encountered Brian; we, coincidentally in time and direction being of the same homeward mind.

As it happened, his presence in the far corner of the lounge bar had been noted on previous evenings. Seemingly absorbed by the contents of a broadsheet newspaper, nearly always he would be unaccompanied. With from time to time, a pen or pencil in use, the assumption was that almost certainly he was busy solving crossword puzzle clues, thus preferring solitude.

For my own part, trips to the 'Horse Chestnut' public house were mostly spent with other 'regulars' in conversation, which, dependent on the subject, had the effect of producing, in state of personal spirit, mostly highs and less frequently, lows. However, as things developed, Brian's arrival on the scene was for me, to have possible consequences affecting a dimension far less well understood.

As, on this occasion, one immediately behind the other we departed the landlord's premises, as a matter of politeness we exchanged pleasantries. It becoming obvious that we would be going the same way, strolling side by side we fell into step, the subject matter of our chat, for no apparent reason quickly settling on years gone by.

Brian Younger, it seemed, had been in my year at the local Grammar School, although, cast as we were into different learning streams and at that time living on different sides of the town, we had never encountered one another. And so it was we now introduced ourselves. Myself by my nickname, Harry.

However, for me, bringing doubt on his assertion were his looks. Surely he was 'just too damn young' to have shared those early schooldays. It was an observation expressed in good nature. But my feeling was that, if he expected acceptance of his claim, surely he would feel obliged to explain his undoubted youthfulness.

To be honest, at first I put the alleged falsehood down to the effect of alcohol in his bloodstream. But, step matching step, as we continued on, in the content of his conversation he was more than able to demonstrate a knowledge clearly only available to one with such first-hand experience. Thus I was finally forced into acceptance of his assertion.

And that was how the subject was broached – 'how come he looked so young? Was it the result of good, clean living – regular exercise, healthy diet and the like? Just *what*, was the reason for such a youthful appearance?'

'But,' he told me, seemingly boasting, 'appearance isn't all. Equally so, my physical stamina matches that of a much younger man.'

Again I felt inclined to blame the drink. 'He'd had a drop too much,' the thought. But it was quickly dispelled. For, surprising me greatly, suddenly he assumed the crouched, 'ready' attitude of an Olympic runner and just as quickly was off, sprinting down the road to the corner shop some 75 yards away. Rapidly reaching his apparent goal, he proceeded to demonstrate great suppleness, nimbly vaulting the side-wall to its frontage, in itself demanding a clearance of some three to four feet in height.

But, on their own, it was not his speed or the height of his jump that shattered prior incredulity. More it was the sheer exuberance he exhibited and energy of youth. To this very day my belief is that no one would believe such a performance from someone of his claimed age.

Then as fast as he had gone, he was returned to my side, again chatting; amazingly his breathing as normal as my own. Truly astounded by the whole performance, I was lost for an answer and immediately thereafter, a question.

"Couldn't have done that last week." – his first words, renewing the subject of our previous conversation – and in so doing, confessing at least some claim to normality. "Not that I've had any practice, you understand. It's just that something rather peculiar has been happening to me lately. It seems so unlikely a story I haven't told anyone else. I didn't think they'd believe me.

But as a contemporary, if you're interested I'd like to tell *you*. You may scoff, nevertheless I must tell someone or I'll go off my head."

"Go on!" I urged, hoping my response sounded convincing. I had no desire to hurt his feelings but, deep down, I felt this might all be just a tall story. Nevertheless, I was prepared to listen.

"Well, Harry," he began, "here I'm hoping that you have not neglected your education, particularly so in regard to new developments in the field of popular physics. For example and crucial to understanding, you will know that a simple definition of 'time' is, the measurement of that which exists between events – agreed?" Here he paused. Then, assuming that it indicated comprehension plus acquiescence and again, attentive disposition, satisfied by my silence he continued.

"Also, Harry, you should know that I'm an horologist, a craftsman of the old school – retired now from the commercial world, you understand, but I am still excited when I come across an old timepiece.

So, I hear you ask, what has all this to do with the subject of our talk? Well... the answer is, everything. For, as much as I myself can understand of the puzzling situation, the reason for my newfound youth cannot possibly be genetic – how could it be? Nor, as I have already told you, is it due to anything I myself have changed in my way of life. Simply put, in the normal way of things it is inexplicable."

And here the pause was accompanied by a lowering of his eyes from mine; he, obviously uncomfortable at the thought of my reaction to what he was about to reveal. "Look, Harry," he continued eventually, now returned to eye contact, "we've been friends – if that's what we are – for only these last few minutes, whilst strolling home. At this early stage of our relationship, nobody would blame you if what I'm about to reveal, leads you to the belief that I'm a raving lunatic. The two of us the other way round, certainly I would doubt your sanity."

So, just what was, the big secret? What was it, that had set him on this strange path of rejuvenation? At this point, I had to admit doubt was overcome by curiosity.

With no comment in return forthcoming, he continued, telling me: "Well, Harry, my predicament, I believe, is somehow related to the workings of a certain stopwatch." And here he halted, no doubt expectant of cynicism. But with, for guidance, nothing other than the bemused look on my face, his words were aptly in answer.

"I know, I know, sounds ridiculous doesn't it? However, if you are prepared to accept, for the moment, that I am **not** out of my mind, and given that I am prepared to offer a practical demonstration – although, as you will understand, without the timepiece concerned there is no purpose to continuing here and now – so I may put forward all the evidence, perhaps you will agree to us meeting again?"

Again he halted, but in vain, as still perplexed by the whole affair, once more I failed to voice an opinion.

"Your agreement," he continued, anxious the subject should not be dropped, "would answer the question as to why I've given you the facts this far. Frankly I need someone's help. More succinctly, I need the assistance of someone educated, someone with an open mind, then also someone with a little time to spare, and not least of all, someone interested enough to listen."

This time leaving no opportunity for answer, he quickly added: "Harry, I would not have told you all this if I did not feel I could trust you. We're obviously of similar learning and background, and I believe that now you may be intrigued enough to want to know more. What do you say?"

Well, what could I say? He was right, I <u>was</u> intrigued. But given, as he said, I had known him for such a short period of time, his story was surely such, that he might **well** be deranged. Nevertheless, he was certainly an intelligent person and his claim, thus far, greatly interesting. And again, the subject scientific or mystical, given the sincerity he displayed, what could I lose?

A pipe dream it may be, but who knows, the possibility was that, like Brian, I too might find the effect of a few years of wear and tear fortuitously dropping away. Consequently, if only out of self-interest, I agreed.

At this juncture, my own path continuing straight on for some further, considerable distance, Brian indicated his need to change direction. In shaking hands in parting, with the both of us retired and widowers, each living alone and neither particularly busy, advised of his home address I agreed to visit him the following morning at ten o'clock.

Following my use of the bell-push, the door was answered promptly. It seemed my host was relieved to see me. The thought was confirmed as after the customary greeting he confessed his fear that following his apparent 'story-telling' of the previous evening, I may well have cried off.

"On the contrary,' I told him, 'I am anxious to hear more and, if that is what is required of me, to be involved." But, of course, firstly there was a pot of tea to be shared.

Later, with the burning issue of the day still to be broached and the used china cleared away, came an awkward silence. It was as though he was waiting for me to ask. Although, as I was there at his invitation, I felt reluctant to do so. However, it seemed I had been oversensitive, for abruptly he apologised for his 'thoughtless lapse of concentration'. Then, again leaving his chair, he moved across the room, targeting a drawer in the impressive sideboard and dresser imposingly positioned on the wall facing the door.

As earlier I had entered the tastefully decorated and furnished room, superbly hand-crafted in dark oak, the quality of the impressive unit and that of its displayed, decorative fine bone-china, was immediately recognised. Deranged or no, Brian most certainly was not short of a bob or two.

Quickly found in the depths of the drawer, it was no ordinary stopwatch and the manner in which it was presented – 'purely for visual examination, of course,' – surely added something to the description of 'uncommonly attractive'.

Certainly it was of the early twentieth century. Carried in a waistcoat pocket and attached by, in matching gold or silver, a fine-link, anchored chain, as worn by gentlemen of that era, it had the looks of an old fob watch.

However, extra to the normal stem-winder was the outstanding difference, the more substantial, operating stem of a stopwatch.

"What do you think of that?" asked my host. "Pretty impressive, eh?"

"Crikey! Yes I should say so," my genuine observation. "Obviously previously owned by someone of affluence and today probably worth quite a bit," I suggested, but with no real knowledge of the market. "Silver isn't it?" I asked – an attempt at covering my ignorance, nevertheless questioning what might be the obvious.

"Quite so," Brian confirmed, "although, considering its true value, surprisingly it cost me very little. I bought it at an auction in a job lot from a jeweller and watchmaker's business in liquidation; apparently as the result of the owner's mysterious disappearance."

"Quite a find," I responded.

"Anyway," Brian continued, "that was some three weeks ago. Since then my world has changed completely," he told me. For it was while he was operating his new find, he further explained, that he discovered its unusual working. Instead of, as expected, running forwards, defying explanation, incredibly it ran backwards.

Now I was really confused and again unable to make comment. Especially so, when despite his earlier promise he refused to demonstrate the veracity of his claim.

"At this stage," as he put it, "too dangerous. For although I have no idea how it came about, it was while it was so running, that the physiological changes to my being seemed to take place. Maybe a freak accident, who knows?" And there he halted, awaiting comment, watching for changes in facial expression. "There, I told you it was unbelievable," he concluded ultimately, assuming the nature of the answer to come to be of ridicule.

"Well, Brian," I answered finally, "you have to admit it does have the ring of a tale from Tolkien. Nevertheless, the proof of the pudding is surely in the eating. So where do we go from here?"

He responded, so it seemed, bluntly, offering me the options of either, with no hard feelings, forgetting the whole thing or, listening to his proposition. I had come this far down the line, I told him and indicated acceptance of the latter course of action.

"OK my friend," he consequently continued, "as I believe you are suggesting, the next step is a demonstration. However, given that I myself, as I said, know little, if anything, of the power involved, the decision as to your part in the operation must be all yours. But you must be prepared perhaps to share the effect. What I mean is, you too may find changes taking place in your own body."

Looking me straight in the eye, there was no mistaking the meaning – he was deadly serious. "Then again I have no idea of the long term effects. This and the possibility that the original happening and the process itself were some sort of accident, are surely factors for sober consideration," he concluded.

As the possible consequences of my inclusion in the experiment were carefully considered, the ensuing quiet was uninterrupted. This was the point of no return. In an attempt to make sense of it all, the pros and cons of the situation needed weighing one against the other. At the heart of my concern was, that given Brian's total sincerity in the matter, 'where would all this end?' But before that, the need was for courage, the courage to leap into the unknown.

As I glanced down to my clasped hands, from the whiteness of the knuckles I realised just how tense I had become, accentuated further by the uneasy sensation of cold sweat on my brow. All I needed to do was say, OK. But somehow, I could find neither courage nor breath. Finally however, normal life-signs returned and hesitatingly I gave him my answer; disappointing him. Nervously, I advised him I needed further time to think things through. Surprisingly he was not upset. Indeed, so he told me, he was relieved that I had not, 'for the sake of personal vanity', simply jumped in at the deep end. "Take as much time as you like," he urged me. "The offer is on hold."

And that was how we parted. Again, the shake of hands indicated our intention of a prolonged friendship, as did our words, we promising to meet for a beer or two in the lounge bar of the 'Horse Chestnut' later that day in the evening.

He did not appear. I waited beyond the usual departure time, but no sign of him. Neither had he been seen earlier. I decided that some urgent matter had cropped up, preventing his keeping the appointment. Not that a continuation of the arrangement had been made, but unusually I thought, neither was he there the following evening.

By the end of that week still he had made no appearance. "Not unusual," was the landlord's response to my enquiry, opposing my own belief. "Sometimes he doesn't come in for a week or two," he explained. But days on, then a matter of weeks, still there was no Brian. Telephone calls went unanswered and thus it was that one morning into the fourth week, unannounced I determined to revisit his home.

"Hasn't been seen for a week or so," as I prepared to desert the front doorbell of my erstwhile co-conspirator, it was the explanation of a helpful, close neighbour.

And so the situation continued, Brian's absence from the scene taken as a sudden call to an ailing relative's bedside, most likely out of town.

But unbeknown to myself, also frustrated in his attempts to contact him, was a nephew – as it turned out Brian's sole, living relative. Eventually, some eight weeks on, he called in the authorities and the house was broken into. Little came of the legal, invasion of privacy. They found no clue to Brian Younger's whereabouts.

Currently, some twelve months on, the mortgage holders having repossessed Brian's home, the house is still up for sale. Totally bemused and distressed, the nephew had been forced into selling off the furniture and effects to pay outstanding debts.

Thus far unrevealed in the telling of this tale, however, is that on the first occasion of entering his missing uncle's home, finding a small parcel addressed to one of his Uncle Brian's friends, he had duly delivered it: a generous gift of a silver stopwatch.

With no note of explanation, it seems the options concerning use or no of the mysterious power of this unusual timepiece once offered to a relative stranger, were to remain on offer.

However, with the curiosity of that friend dampened by lack of explanation as to the donor's disappearance – and incidentally, that of its unfortunate previous owner – the watch and whatever power it may or may not hold, remains perhaps fortunately, further untried. For, with its new owner of too cowardly disposition, to this very day it lies buried at the bottom of an old tea-chest of knick-knacks, itself tucked away in some shadowy corner of my loft.

III
GIFTED

Thinking about it, I suppose I always did have the ability. Although to this very day, no one else is aware. Indeed, it was many years on before even I myself recognised it for what it was.

For, as a child, I did not think it unusual that when someone spoke, I could mouth exactly their words simultaneously. It was so natural, it did not occur to me that I actually knew beforehand what they were about to say.

In the first instance it came about because, as the oldest child of three, I loved tantalising my siblings, especially my younger brother. And finding that it upset him, it was a childish habit in which I delighted.

As later I matured and the fad of teasing deserted me, it gradually became apparent that, beyond the spoken word, increasingly I was, as I believed, hearing voices. In a small gathering these manifested themselves as nothing more than an extra buzz to that of normal conversation. But even so, by concentrating hard on those of a particular wavelength, whilst filtering out others, individual thoughts would sometimes become readable. However, not so in a large crowd where the process was almost impossible. On the other hand, in managing the situation, like a radio operator I now find I can control the volume, up or down – at stressful times, thankfully blanking it all out.

And so it was, albeit in the beginning unknowingly, I was graced with a distinct advantage in life over my fellow man. However, in later life, rarely would it be utilised to selfish end. Although I would confess that in my chosen livelihood of face-to-face selling, helping to turn a crust into a slice of cake, it was often used to advantage,

However, in the successful courting and marrying of the most desirable girl in my circle of friends, taking advantage of my gift, had other would-be suitors been aware, might just be put at the door of unsporting behaviour. Now, Annabel and I have two lovely children, but not one with the ability to read thoughts – perhaps for them a blessing. For, as in all things, sad to relate there is a downside to all of this, illustrated by the one time it could be said I put the gift to evil use.

Although at first perhaps considered a blessing, so rapidly it became obvious that there were times, when in probing the silent contents of an individual's mind, one would learn of matters perhaps best left undiscovered – as might become clear from the following record of recent, unhappy experience.

Given the relatively contented state of my marriage, surprisingly the storm that might test the strength of its foundation, was to come from the least likely of directions. Slim, pretty in the face and with naturally blonde hair other women would die for, Emma is my wife's niece.

I first encountered her when, a year before our wedding, as an engaged couple we visited, on the east coast, Annabel's sister and her family. As the taxi bringing us from the local railway station arrived at their delightful, country cottage, recently home from a day of learning, Emma, in school uniform, stood waiting on the doorstep with her mother and younger brother.

Of the threesome, in particular Emma's radiant, open smile of welcome seemed, to me, less reserved. Then, in the same way, immediately following what was only a shake of hands from the other two members of the family, by Emma was replaced by an affectionate hug; and this, for both her obviously adored aunt and surprisingly, myself – bringing a blush to the cheeks.

At the time she was going on twelve, but even then, with sparkling conversation and wit exhibited a maturity far beyond her years. Thereafter, seemingly she would spend all her available spare time in my company.

And thus it was we became great pals. Although until her family moved house – returning them here to her mother's hometown – visits, each to the other's home by the two sisters, were limited to those of relatively short duration, time when again Emma and I would have the opportunity to renew our friendship.

Then, at her favourite aunt and uncle's wedding, she was, of course, a very willing bridesmaid; when, despite the occasion, again I would find myself willingly enticed into the now teenage Emma's company, who with cheeks blooming, would all but steal away the thunder of the bride.

Today Emma has a husband of her own and two beautiful children and in all the time between, the number of our meetings can be counted on the digits of two hands. But when we do meet, it's always with the same smiles, the same hug and no matter how short a time, a lively conversation full of interest. Indeed, with Emma and her family living on the opposite side of town, these days I see more of her husband Craig; he and I meeting at a prearranged venue for a game of snooker once a week.

"Will you to take this parcel of material to Emma's for me, please, Harry?" Annabel rarely missed the chance to visit her niece's home, but this week her evenings were to be taken up at the local technical college, where in separate classes, respectively she was learning about woodworking, re-upholstery and interior decoration. Bought especially for Emma from our local market, delivery of this promised acquisition – the result of an earlier discussion between aunt and niece on the two latter subjects of learning – was urgent I was told. 'Could I find time to drop it into her?'

I knew that Craig was with his local, amateur rugby team at an international event in France, away for a few days – so no snooker tonight. My mother-in-law would be babysitting the children I was informed, leaving me a free evening and no excuse for refusal. Consequently I promised to do as I was asked, telling Annabel not to expect me for tea, since I would take advantage of the situation and work over, visiting Emma later.

Here, essential to understanding is that, perhaps because in my job during the day it found overuse, my habit was, on departing the office always to turn off my 'extrasensory receiver'. With trust being an integral part of both marriage and parenthood, I considered there was little need of it at home.

"Harry. How lovely to see you!" As always, the sincerity of the greeting was shown no less so in the accompanying hug and kiss to the cheek. But this evening, as the warmth of the lithesome Emma's greeting – both in word and disconcertingly from her body – permeated my being, I was visited by a strange, but otherwise familiar thrill. Strange, in that it was foreign to previous occasions of our meeting; familiar, in that, delightfully, it was one I had known since the early days of puberty.

Emma thanked me for delivering her prized parcel and as she put it to one side, asked: "I was about to have a small sherry, will you join me?"

"Well," I explained, "I didn't intend staying but... well... er... OK. Yes I will, thank you. Why not?" Was acceptance of the invitation prompted by a sudden rush of blood to the head or, truth be known, to the loins? Deep inside I sensed a warning of something wrong in the situation. But tonight, strangely, there was an undeniable attraction in the flaxen-haired Emma.

Perhaps it was the way that, after filling our glasses, in ladylike manner she firstly perched herself on the edge of the table, then in the way of a pendulum, seductively swung her shapely, stockingless legs back and forth, the pointed toes of her diminutive, bare feet adding to the rousing of my senses.

Resuming the tapestry work with which presumably she had been engaged before I arrived, she began talking about her two young boys: Scott, now three and a half, and just four months old, Aaron, the latest arrival. "Both were in bed," she explained, issuing the weary sigh of a busy young mother. "Both, hopefully fast asleep."

In what seemed no time at all our glasses were empty and the obviously now-revived young mother, in no mood for accepting refusals, attended to refills, afterwards resuming her seat on the edge of the table. With her eyes then rarely leaving her needlework, the subject of conversation duly remained centred on the family.

Time passed quickly and with news and welfare of other members of our respective clans well and truly covered, came yet another refill. Voicing no objection to this obvious self-indulgence, for my own part I would now confess to allowing the drink to compound the daring of the situation. Whatever the effect it was having on Emma, without reading her thoughts one could only guess - which strangely enough, had not occurred to me. However, increasingly she allowed talk to become of our own, two private lives, prompted, of course, by my fast-becoming-deliberate questions.

Now considered in retrospect, questions such as, "So how come Craig gets all this time to himself?" mostly were without any idea of where they would lead. But doubtless they were attempts to provoke inner doubts in the mind of the former fun-loving, young mother; in particular prompting her to question her part in the married relationship.

Then in pursuing the theme, I painted a picture of a spouse with seemingly no bounds to his free time. "I mean to say, he's out with me at least one evening a week. Then there's his rugger at the weekend. And now this trip to France. With life for you now dominated so much more by the boys and the house, I don't suppose you have much time to yourself, eh?" All in all, the suggestion she was intended to consider, was that clearly she was entitled to more freedom of her own.

Thinking back, though at the time it was given no thought, this was not the behaviour of a happily married man. More, it was that of a young, single man, attempting to lure a young lady away from a rival, in the hope of taking her into his own lascivious arms.

But in this case, all could be taken as in good fun. After all, here the other man was her husband and my best friend. The question was, did Emma see it that way? Or did she somehow understand that behind all of this, there was some hidden, selfish reason?

'But what was I doing? What was I about?' Certainly eating away at my moral fibre, the drink was playing its part. The daydream coursing through my soul was the possibility that Emma felt the same and in the event, we might illicitly meet, away from the family, on our own, alone.

I knew I had absolutely no right to think about her in this way. But in sudden realisation I was seeing Emma for what she really was – a beautiful, desirable woman. And in that moment, I silently blasphemed, calling on the good 'Lord' to witness and affirm the attractiveness of this woman.

"Well," she said, "you're quite right. As much as I love Craig and the children, it would be nice to get out on my own now and then. Not that we don't get out and about, visiting friends and the like. But that's always together, as a family. Yes, it is something I've been thinking about lately. If only to give me a break from the children, I do need more freedom. After all, I do need to recharge my batteries from time to time. I'll talk it over with Craig when he gets back. I know he will be in agreement."

'Other than the alcohol, there had to be a reason,' I told myself, 'for the obvious rise in her colour and the almost shy look she gave me, then afterwards, the way she quickly avoided my obviously lingering gaze.'

With my senses in turmoil and conscience pricking, seemingly without conscious command, telepathy came into play, taking on a life of its own, recklessly scanning Emma's subconscious for hidden messages.

Realisation brought disgust at such a despicable act and I attempted to curb it. But the effect of the sherry again weakened any resolve I may have had, the effort proving useless. I was almost in panic. I knew she knew nothing of my thoughts, but I was afraid body language would give me away. Whatever happened, I wanted nothing to spoil our relationship.

The thought occurred to suggest purely a platonic meeting, for a coffee sometime, or – perhaps much too forward – for a drink in the evening. But, as I attempted to return to a good and proper manner, the struggle to block out her private thoughts sent my own into turmoil. All I could think of now, was escape – away from the temptation. I had to get home before something happened I would regret.

However, in one vital respect it was too late. I hoped it was my imagination, but, coming over loud and clear telepathically, was a thought I knew Emma would never want made public. I'm sure I rouged as I realised that in Emma's mind was, an evening rendezvous with her handsome uncle – yes, incredibly with me.

I made an honest attempt to leave. "You know, Emma, I'm sorry but I really must be going," I told her, rising to my feet.

"Oh, what a shame," she said, quickly slipping her slim, skirted bottom off the table.

Then, my hand taken in hers, with sultry eyes questioning mine, she asked in matter of fact manner: "But before you go, wouldn't you like to take a peek at the children? You haven't seen them for some time. I know they're asleep, but if you take your shoes off and we creep up quietly, they won't be disturbed. Come on," she urged, "you've got time. Just slip off your shoes and follow me."

With seemingly no escape route, half-heartedly I followed her bidding then her person. As it happened she would have it no other way, she again taking my hand in a firm grasp – one that I read in her roguish mind as: 'Oh no you don't, Harry. No way are you going home just yet!'

As 'shackled' together, 'prisoner' and 'jailor' reached the top of the stairs, in linked tandem I was led across the wide landing to the master bedroom, then across its plush carpet to the closed door of the adjoining nursery. There, with the index finger of her free hand to her lips, Emma indicated the need for silence then slowly turned the doorknob before gently pushing open the door, leaving a small gap through which to peek.

As one body close behind the other we stood together watching Emma's wondrous brood in energy-replenishing sleep, we were careful not to wake them. All of this time, standing in front of me Emma held my hand firmly in hers, pulling it and with it me, close up behind her, my head, for a view, dropping alongside hers, our cheeks, thrillingly all but touching.

Moments on, she signalled her intent, then silently but securely reclosed the door. The task complete, again she offered no release for my hand, in turn allowing no room for bodily escape as then she twisted her lithe, warm body around to face me, her questioning eyes meaningfully on mine. Then, fully aware of what she was about, she made a deliberate act of parting her lips, slowly the tip of a teasing tongue moistening them sensuously.

There was little need for the reading of thoughts. For her uncle, matters were hardening below, and our close proximity would have left no doubt in Emma's mind as to my bodily desire. As I heard the turn of a key behind her, then the dropping of tumblers in the lock, my fate, I knew was sealed. There was far too much pent-up passion in the embrace and kiss that followed to suggest otherwise.

And with any doubts about the irresponsibility of my actions quashed involuntarily, with my secret channel to Emma's thoughts still open, I knew exactly the degree of urgency there lay in her cry for me to take her. For it was for then and there.

Thank goodness for the baby's cry and with it the breaking of the spell. Fortunately, the rude reality of our individual responsibilities was suddenly forced upon us and with embarrassed utterances we broke apart; Emma, whilst tidying herself, also quickly unlocking the door to the nursery.

To say that, as earlier she had suggested the trip upstairs, thoughts of a sexual encounter had been there to read in Emma's mind, would be untrue. However, through the maelstrom of confusion there in her mind at the time, were wild, unshackled thoughts which included her uncle; daydreams that had obviously visited before, and within that, no matter how little, most definitely there was an element of intent.

It might be said that in allowing the situation to develop as far as it did, in being the elder of the would-be erring couple, I was the more to blame. However, in mitigation I would suggest that without the God-given ability to read Emma's thoughts, matters may never have reached the stage they indeed did.

For me, guilt usually shouts loud and clear on my face. However, how the following morning, faced with the family I avoided giving the game away – as curtailed as it was – I had no idea; especially so to Annabel. Certainly I felt guilty – guilty as sin.

And how could I ever face Craig again? Well, as I told myself, the fact was, I couldn't. But then, how to explain the sudden distancing of myself from him, and of course from Emma and the boys? And just what, was I to do about Emma herself? Obviously I was totally obsessed with her and as I gathered from her behaviour and own private thoughts, she too with me. Last evening had certainly been a close shave for both of us. The question was, would I be able to leave her alone? And what about Emma herself? To satisfyingly bring her daydreams to fruition, would she be tempted to try again?

Now, prior to leaving the house for work, so worried was I that Annabel suspected something, I broke the golden rule. Anxious to secretly learn of anything untoward in her mind, deviously I switched on the receiver. Unlike formal radio operation, thought-reading, as might be understood, gives no warning of an impending message. So it was that, as immediately before departing I took in the full meaning of my wife's thoughts, I felt my jaw drop and the colour of my face turn to scalding hot, deep scarlet.

For, stupefying me, certainly my activities were dominating Annabel's mind, as immediately preceding their open expression, her thoughts read: 'I must remind Harry to deliver that material to Emma's this evening.'

God! Had it all been a dream? It must have been. How else could Annabel's thoughts be interpreted? Hopefully, the reaction — as she saw it, to her words and the handing over of the parcel concerned — was mistaken for sudden, guilty remembrance of a half-forgotten promise on her husband's part.

Left to the discretion of the reader is, what happened at Emma's home later that evening? And in any possible, future recriminations, would there, indeed, be need for mitigating circumstances, gifted or not?

IV
OH, EMMA!

(Sequel to 'Gifted')

"Haven't seen you for a while, Craig. Is everything alright?" It was true, I'd seen neither hide nor hair of him since his rugby-club trip to France. Mind you, if he had access to my dreams concerning Emma, his wife, my wife's niece, the current lack of contact might be understandable. Although, more likely he would have come round straight away, to no doubt 'punch my lights out' – one good reason for not ringing him before this.

"Look, Harry, I don't know quite how to tell you this, but I've discovered Emma's having an affair." The blunt revelation completely knocked the wind out of me. I was totally flabbergasted and not least of all, worried. And, in his response, the question of our own wavering friendship had been completely ignored – at least for the moment.

What exactly was it he had found out? Then again, even if somehow he did know of my feelings for Emma, strictly speaking nothing had happened between us. Sure, in my dream it had been a close call but, parting us from our passionate embrace at the last minute, the waking baby's cries rudely reminded us of our respective families and moral responsibilities, returning us to our senses. Or so it was for

42

myself – after all, Emma was there only in my imagination. But then, had he found out about my actual visit to his home the following evening?

Inevitably overcome by self-concern, finally the mind-fogging effect of guilt cleared away and the bull taken by the horns, after a deep breath, I asked: "But what's happened, Craig? I can't believe what you are telling me. Emma? – an affair? It's just not possible. You're such a happy pair, a lovely little family. Tell me, what's happened?"

"Well, Harry, amongst other things, very unlike Emma, she's been talking in her sleep. A couple of nights after I got back from my trip to France, I was woken by her excessive tossing and turning in bed – and from her murmuring it was all too obvious she was having an erotic dream."

During the whole of this evening's telephone encounter with my friend, such was the shock to the system, not once had I attempted to utilise my mind-reading ability. With me since childhood, not even the closest members of the family knew about it; and as I was anxious for it to remain a secret, usually my in-built 'receiver' was deliberately switched off at the end of each working day.

But now, with a jealous husband to contend with, and personal interest involved, I might have been tempted to try and read Craig's mind to discover just how much he knew. However, in attempting to stay ahead of current developments in the conversation, the continuous racing of my own mind left no real opportunity to do so.

"Did she mention a name?" I asked, concealing self-interest as best I could.

"No, Harry, none at all. But, then again, a lot of what was said was mumbled, most of it unintelligible."

Then, following a pause for deliberation and interpreting this as a cry for help, I began to offer my honest opinion of his dilemma, telling him: "Well, Craig, if that's the sum total of the evidence…"

"No, no, Harry, not at all," he interrupted, countering my obvious attempt to dismiss his claim as of total imagination. "That's not the whole of it. Cutting a long story short, without telling her, I consequently decided to stay off work, during that day secretly watching the house."

Doubtless my face registered surprise but, situated as it was some few miles away at the other end of a telephone line, Craig, of course, was unaware. Nevertheless, he quite obviously caught my mood, as he heard an involuntary gasp of, "Crikey!", which apparently had much the same effect on him, he defensively offering: "Look Harry, what else was I to do? The morning after her turbulent dream, although on the face of it jokingly, I challenged her. She, of course, rubbished the whole matter, but her reaction gave her away. Red-faced and nervous it was obvious she was hiding something."

In my guilty mind the call made in my erotic dream and, as innocent as it had been, the actual visit the following evening, were one in the same, to which, this far, all the evidence pointed. But suddenly here was a new, unexpected twist to the tale. For now, following on, he was relating an eyewitness account of a lunchtime liaison between his wife and a stranger, a man.

Apparently, having openly arranged for a baby-sitter so that she might do some shopping alone, after leaving the bus in town she had calmly walked to a quiet side-street where, obviously pre-arranged, she was picked up by a car driven by the aforementioned mystery man.

Supposedly to swallow his hurt Craig paused, then quickly finalised his report with the fact that in earlier abandoning his car to follow her on foot, he had denied himself the means to follow them. And unfortunately being some distance away, neither had he been close enough to read the registration number, nor indeed, see the face of the driver.

"Craig, Craig, I just don't know what to say," I confessed, despite then conversely suggesting that the whole thing might be perfectly innocent. Then in an attempt to progress the conversation further, I asked: "So what's happening now, old chap?"

"Well, Harry," revealed the sad voice, "I again challenged Emma, asking her just what was going on. The net result was that, without answer, taking the children with her she up and left me. I've since discovered they are all at her mother's. That was nearly a week ago, and they are still there."

"So what are you doing about it?" I asked, showing genuine concern.

"Well, to be honest, Harry, what with her disloyal behaviour and deceit, I'm still very angry with Emma. I do miss the children and certainly I would like things returned to where they were before. But until I know just what has been going on behind my back, I don't really want Emma back. That she is keeping quiet, you must agree, certainly does not act in her favour."

He stopped, waiting for my reaction, but with none forthcoming he continued, informing me: "What I have done though, Harry, might not meet with your approval, but, with no idea of what else to do, perhaps recklessly I've set the wheels in motion already."

I waited in silence, expecting him to carry on. But after an inordinately long break in the conversation, hiding natural apprehension I prompted him, with feigned impatience asking: "So are you going to tell me, or must I drag it out of you?"

I had an uneasy feeling that something was wrong. Something in his voice suggested irrational behaviour. Naturally, the man was disturbed by events. Suddenly his otherwise contented life was under threat. The problem was he was floundering in a sea of jealousy, unable to find a way of saving his family from breaking up. But no, that was not quite the case. For, whatever it was, he had a plan of action and it was already under way.

Still Craig remained mute. The opportunity to lean on my thought-reading ability presented itself and nervously I activated the inbuilt receiver, only for the whole procedure to be interrupted by the sound of weeping at the other end of the line.

"What is it, old chap?" I asked sympathetically, halting the mental process. "Please don't go on so. I know things may seem bad at the moment, but I'm sure things will turn out OK eventually. Just you wait and see."

I was attempting to pour oil on troubled waters but, in my heart of hearts I guessed that with so much fire and passion involved, unintentionally I might just be feeding a potential inferno.

"I don't think so, Harry," he said, suddenly breaking his silence. "You see, I've done something unforgivable. I sent Emma a note, telling her that if she did not return the children immediately, I would make it my business to discover the name of her lover and... well... at the very least, put him in hospital." The hesitation had been deliberate. Without actually descending to the depths of describing the animal brutality he intended for this trouble-causing interloper, nevertheless the intent of inflicting maximum injury and pain was accentuated. And when, afterwards, he also revealed the probable involvement of 'one or two boys from the rugby club', it was obvious he was deadly serious.

"Apart from that," he continued, "I've had some little success in finding out who the bastard is. Apparently, one evening while I was away, Emma had a male visitor. He was seen by one of my nosey neighbours. She informed me when she came to the house to see if there was anything she could do for me, having somehow discovering Emma's desertion.

"Because of the parking restrictions outside the house, his car, she told me, had been parked around the corner. Living opposite the junction, she only caught sight of it when, whoever it was, drove away. Unfortunately, with no real reason to do so, she had taken no note of the registration number; although she did remember it was a new car, with, she believed, a 'W' prefix. Added to that her description seemed to match that of my own day-time sighting of the car in which Emma drove away.

"You yourself drive a Peugeot 406, don't you, Harry?" The question knocked me backwards, such was the shock. "And also, as I recall, the colour is metallic silver, isn't it? And isn't yours a 'W' registration, too? Certainly there must be a fair few like that on the road. Popular car, eh?" I prayed he expected no answer. My voice, I knew, would fail me.

It was obvious the sharp-eyed neighbour had witnessed my own, innocent visit to see Emma. But the car seen by Craig in the town? No, certainly that was not mine. Within this opposing mix, thinking was confused and having this far revealed nothing of my own visit to see Emma while he was away, rightly or wrongly I determined to remain out of the running for the part of wife-stealer.

"Anyway," continued a now recovered Craig, "all is not lost, I have another clue to follow up. From a sticker in the rear window of the car my inquisitive neighbour also remembered the supplier's name – memorable for her in that her son just happens to work there. She also noticed that the rear bumper was in need of attention. With her son's help, I wouldn't mind betting I'll be able to trace the owner fairly easily. Then we'll find out just what he's been up to with my wife," a possibly-cuckolded husband declared jubilantly.

The opportunity to explain my own innocent part in the whole of this unfortunate matter was long past. Foolishly I had let things develop too far. Now there was a huge lump in my throat and in my stomach, one of sickening lead. At the same time, the feeling beneath my feet was of the ground opening up. By senselessly remaining quiet, I had dug myself a black, yawning pit, from which I could see no escape.

Now, with the handset of the telephone nestled cosily in its cradle, and Craig left to his own devices, malevolently going about the business of finding his wife's alleged lover, and my car currently undergoing repairs to the rear bumper, unusually housed in the service department of Peugeot's, local main dealer, I sit here, the victim of relatively innocent dreams, my otherwise perfect world about to be dashed on the jagged rocks of dishonest intent. How gifted can one be? 'Oh, Emma!'

V
SNAPDRAGON

That King Arthur and his adviser, the mystical Merlin, had some kind of pact and that it involved the art of magic, to anyone familiar with this legend of old England is no small secret, including myself. And yet, in all these sixty odd years of living the thought never occurred. Then again, there was no real reason why it should – that is until now.

Strangely involved in the revealment of a weird, modern-day coincidence, is the advance of computer technology and in its marketing the use of brand names and logos.

For it was during a recent and rare visit to an old friend when, delighted with the opportunity to show me the results of his new hobby, making me aware of another aspect of magic – but this of the 21st century – he started to demonstrate the unbelievably fantastic capabilities of his latest, electronic acquisition.

Being of the same time-worn generation as myself, he knew that I would be interested in his work of upgrading the quality of prints of old family photographs. Needless to report, some in sepia, the originals were monotone. Not to dwell too heavily on the technical aspects involved, but, in particular aided by the very latest digital printer and on-screen facilities –

allowing choice of image, change of size and improvement of quality – results, I can report, were spectacular.

Within the power of this latest miracle of science, I was told, was the ability to patch and heal imperfections. These may have been the result of poor technique on the part of the original photographer or some fault in the original photographic equipment, or indeed, in the subject itself.

As an example, I was shown a fifty-year-old portrait of a now deceased relative, whose smile on the original print was marred by the obviously premature extraction of a prized, front tooth.

Digitally treated on screen, the unsightly gap, with the benefit of no bill from the dentist, was expertly filled with a matching incisor. 'A truly remarkable feat,' I congratulated my friend.

Plaudits and obvious interest motivated him into revealing yet another inner secret of this sanctum, he choosing to show me a recently taken picture of his two dogs at play in the local park. "Unfortunately, it had been almost impossible to contain it to just this frolicking pair," I was told, "since neighbouring, battling hounds annoyingly were intent on getting in on the act.'

However, the snap I was shown, it seemed, was only partly spoiled. As momentarily she had dashed through the already activated lens, top right the hindquarters and flagging tail of an excited Alsatian bitch had found their way into the picture, marring a perfect result. Unfortunately, a simple cut to remove evidence of her presence would have created a print of unacceptable shape.

"But," my friend revealed, "all was not lost. All that was required was a little time and patience working on a computer print."

In demonstration, sliding and clicking the hand-operated 'mouse', my expert tutor, with deft movements of the on-screen cursor, slowly but certainly merged the image of the unwanted canine into the background, until finally, as if by magic, she was no more. "Truly amazing technology," my candid assessment of the proceedings.

It was then, as he printed off another copy, that my host decided to disclose even more, telling his long-time confidante: "But, Harry, the story doesn't end there." He seemed hesitant to continue but, again the interest shown in my face drew him on, he further revealing: "I wouldn't want this to get about, old son, but there are aspects to all this that do not make sense. I'm sure when I've given you the facts you'll think I'm imagining things. I wish it was the case, but the evidence against is growing." Needless to relate, intrigued and anxious to learn more I urged him on, in so doing promising my full and earnest attention.

"To tell the truth, Harry, the whole business has been worrying me no end," he confessed. "I daren't tell Barbara, she'll think I'm finally off my head. She's not a bad wife, but she always did think some of my ideas strange."

"Carry on," I implored him, indicating interest and with it my wish to help. "Tell me all about it."

"Well, as I said," he continued hesitantly, "I don't think anyone else will believe this but, nevertheless here goes." He stopped to pull from his trouser pocket a crisp, white handkerchief and with it wiped the developing sweat from his brow before further explaining:

"Harry, you saw what I did to remove the dog from the photograph, but what you don't know and what you may ridicule, is that the day following my original work on the print, the same Alsatian bitch was hit by a lorry, killing her outright. Now before you say anything," he added quickly, forestalling any judgement I might make, "please hear me out."

Only then did he pause, checking my reaction to his plea. Then, sure of a polite hearing, he carried on. "I know! I know! It's a ridiculous assumption that the two things are connected. In fact on first hearing the owner's sad news, nothing was further from my thoughts. Neither would it have ever occurred to me except for another happening of the same nature, then, even more distressing, a third."

Again he halted, searching my face for ridicule or, as he might expect from an old pal, at least a look of sympathy. For either he was telling tall stories – but that was not his way – or he was losing his mind, or, at the very least, he was sincere in his belief of the happenings. Whatever, I decided to keep my own counsel, at least until all the evidence was in. Thus it was indicated for him to continue.

"As I said, Harry, two more fatal occurrences have since followed other work of this nature; the first involving my next door neighbour's cat, Fluff.

Again I had been demonstrating my new equipment to the cat's owner, Bill. Afterwards, impressed with its capabilities he fetched a photograph he had taken a few days earlier. It was of his wife sunning herself in the garden. He asked if, as a favour, I could take out the small, blurred image in the foreground.

As in spotting an innocent bird and making her move, it was an unintentional record of the hyperactive Fluff, as she too, in the same way of the unfortunate dog before her, had dashed through the open aperture of the camera. Naturally enough, I obliged.

Next day the cat was gone. A spayed cat and thus a contented homebird, never before had the beloved Fluff deserted the home. A few days later, her poor, battered body

was found in the gutter of the main road, half a mile away –
again, apparently the result of a road accident.

Then there was the most disturbing case of all. And again
this happened before I realised there might be some strange
connection with my work. As it happened I had been cleaning
up the image on some holiday photos taken by myself in
Thailand last year. I had spent a great deal of time setting up
one in particular, outside a very attractive Buddhist temple. I
had managed to persuade a number of young monks to set a
pose in the foreground of my chosen view. All told, this would
have been one of my best efforts ever.

However, later, I discovered that unfortunately I had
reckoned without the interference of a reflected shaft of light,
the result of, in the last split-second of clicking the shutter, the
fast-setting sun striking one of the ornate, gold-leafed figures
sited at the side of the building, itself outside the chosen
image. Thus it was that, in later putting the picture to rights,
there was nothing for it but to lose, amongst other things, some
of my eager, orange-robed crowd."

And here my friend halted, strangely troubled, his sad
eyes dropping away from mine.

"Perhaps it would be better not to burden you further,
Harry," he ended his silence.

"No, go on," I pressed him, now fully intrigued and
anxious to learn the full story.

"Well," he continued, "if you're sure, Harry? And the
reason I say that, is as much for my own face-saving as it is for
certainly disturbing you further."

Again he paused, the question repeated in his look. But
with assent signalled, he set about the conclusion of his tale,
explaining: "You may know, Harry, I have relatives in
Thailand – the same ones we visited last year. We're in fairly
regular correspondence and from time to time they send us the

'Bangkok Post'. Well, not to waste your time, it seems that shortly after my computer work on the photo in question, as reported in that newspaper's news columns, that very same temple caught fire, with the consequence that, in an attempt to save the revered, old building, a number of monks tragically lost their lives."

All through this disturbing revelation, I had held my peace, silently watching his age-lined face. Confirming total belief in his own complicity in the tragedy, there registered was complete distress. Finally he raised his sad eyes slowly up from the floor to meet mine. Full of tears, seemingly they were seeking understanding and forgiveness.

Old friends or not, we both understood the choice available to me. I could console him and show compassion or, as he probably feared, I might ridicule the whole matter, crushing his spirit further.

To be perfectly honest, it did seem that coincidence took a large hand in all that he had described and thinking objectively, I could see no real connection in the happenings concerned. 'But how to tell him?'

"Look, old chap," I began, "I have no doubt at all that you are genuinely worried about all this, but let me put a proposition to you.

Firstly, I can't tell you one way or the other whether you are to blame. My good sense tells me, not. But who knows? So here's what I propose…"

I have no idea how I persuaded him – or indeed myself. But one way or the other, the mystery may soon be solved – although, perhaps not the mysticism. For in relating this story, there may be detected an air of finality, given that the photograph 'doctored' today by my friend, was of myself.

And, although perhaps having no bearing whatsoever on matters, for the record, my friend's name just happens to be

Arthur – and bizarrely, though perhaps merely a coincidence, the brand name emblazoned on his computer equipment reads, 'Merlin'.

VI
TURNING UP
or - CONFESSIONS OF A 'RABBIT'

I thought hard and long over a title for this piece. Eventually, however, direct thinking was abandoned. As was so on other, similar occasions of blank mind, it was supposed that something would hopefully 'turn up'.

As those familiar with its intricacies will attest, within the labyrinth of component words and phrases comprising the English language, lies buried a minefield of multiple meaning. Needless to say, exact interpretation is essential to perfect understanding.

Allaying readers' fears, it is not necessary here to cover the complete catalogue of those to be gathered from the eventual choice of labelling. Suffice it to say that, for purposes here, its usage at the end of the opening paragraph to this story, says it all. However, further understanding requires some small knowledge of sport and an open mind.

On a personal front, humankind's obsession with sport has always been found to be puzzling. Healthy competition and of course, the benefit of essential exercise of the body are, in today's busy world, both understood as worthwhile use of leisure time. But the main motivation, doubtless, will be the improvement of performance standards: running even faster, jumping higher and longer, etcetera, etcetera – to some, the be all and end all of life itself.

But, to this mere mortal, even stranger are the antics of those who consider that winning is everything. Not here intended for debate but, as a personal observation on the matter, if such a philosophy is the one to follow, certainly there will be millions of would-be winners leading extraordinarily unhappy lives. Surely then, more satisfying is the act of participation, and the knowledge that, win or lose, one has done one's best. Then, for some, sport also allows that which may not be attainable in other walks of life – the opportunity to grow self-esteem and within that, the bettering of one's position in the pecking order – perhaps itself at the heart of the need to win. But a view of a wider picture almost certainly uncovers an otherwise hidden objective – in civilised society the provision of a relatively harmless outlet for inborn, animal aggression – offsetting the warring instinct.

And so, for whatever of these reasons, three times a week my friend Tom and I, both keen golfers, sometimes in the company of others, will set off down 'the first' together. Although, in that without fail, our individual drives normally finish on opposite sides of the fairway – mine some fifty yards behind that of my playing companions and probably to be found in deep, unplayable 'rough' – our activities, surely, can hardly be described as together.

Whatever, addicted to the game, to those outside our 'diseased' circle we are of a mentality difficult to understand. However, for those fated to witness regular performances, the only possible answer is that without doubt we are of a masochistic tendency. For such irrational behaviour, what other sensible explanation could there be?

In evidence of this reputation, here offered is a definition said to be from the scathing tongue of a golf widow – one with which, apparently, no one has yet been prepared to argue. Not that there is any answer to such a great truth.

Thus we are described as, 'of their own volition, a group of grown men, armed with implements of a design totally unsuitable for the purpose, inexplicably to be found, in all weathers, regularly knocking the hell out of a defenceless, little white ball, mindlessly attempting to project it over terrain better left to the creatures of the wild, unceasingly chasing it from one small hole to another'.

Seriously however, it is a game demanding total dedication, with regular practice an absolute essential to holding form. For, it is an uncomfortable fact of life that, however well one plays today, tomorrow surely will be different – an expected and accepted phenomenon of the sport. So much so that, at times of lowered spirit, gatherings are to be found in futile, philosophical debate, attempting to identify the cause of poor play.

Amusingly, there are those inclined to lay blame at the door of outside agencies. Consider, for example, the inconsiderate earthworm, which in exiting its home, unfairly pops up on the line of a simultaneous putt. Then there is the unnecessary calling of one crow to another, a totally unnecessary event destined to destroy concentration and undoubtedly one of the reasons for hitting a ball off line.

Always playing hell with one's game, also there is the weather to contend with. Like, 'why wasn't that damned tornado of a wind blowing against when one's opponent teed off?' And, the angry reason given for a 'duffed' shot - "it was playing into that damned sun that made me look up too soon". And so on, from many an unhappy player, offerings to explain unsatisfactory performances, a plethora of 'unquestionable' excuses.

But then, held by the author as the truth of the matter, there is the ultimate extenuating circumstance – though one described by cynics as rubbish. However, in another aspect of the phenomenon, these same non-believers may be found not quite so doubting. For, who would doubt the faithful wife and mother's claim that, where her husband and growing sons are concerned, she is responsible for feeding 'the inner man'?

And who is to say that we are not indeed, part physical, part spiritual. Thus, with humankind being of two parts, the more philosophical answer given for poor sporting performance might well be that, on the day, unfortunately one part decided to stay away. And following my own, regular ignominious defeats at Tom's hands, all that might be said, is that sadly deserting me – leaving me to my lonely, 'long-eared burrowing' activities – it seems that being fond of a good laugh, the part of me that knows how to play golf, somewhat mischievously preferred not to turn up, yet again!

VII
LOOKING GOOD

When in my moral upbringing my grandmother used what she considered 'a little white lie', she would never know just how close she was to the truth. For it was her habit to chide me for my untruths, promising that my earlobes would grow bigger by the lie. Neither did she, so I believe, understand the full process involved.

So how is it that in this respect I now claim greater understanding than that revered soul? Well, the truth of the matter is, its coming has taken a lifetime of gazing into the mirror at my reflection – or more so, its changing. And over the years, like anyone with an ounce of self-love, I've done a great deal of that. But, almost because of the regularity of so doing, exacerbated by the slow pace of the process, the clues leading to the basis of this tale were very nearly missed.

But then they may well have been spotted many years earlier as, privileged to view photographs of him at a younger age, I witnessed the facial changes in my step-father as he grew older, in total disbelief of the changes. That is not to say the phenomenon is unique to that honoured gentleman alone. Indeed no. If there is any substance in the belief, it is true for each and every one of us.

Enough then of the preamble. What now is needed is an explanation of how all this came about, allowing judgement of the credibility in the substance of this narrative.

But firstly I would ask you, the reader, to take a look at your own reflection in the mirror. Given that this is intended for adult reading, then already you will be of an age to have weathered a number of life's physical and psychological storms. And if you have followed the normal path into adulthood, doubtless you will have encountered a sexual partner - some perhaps more than one – some pleasurable, some perhaps not so.

Now, the inspection completed, the question to answer with honesty is, over time have there been any changes of note? – not those resulting from self-abuse, physical combat and the like, nor indeed those due to weathering or otherwise legitimately attributed to the natural process of ageing.

No, more to be searched out is the appearance of new, permanent blemishes or, changes in shape of particular features. An honest appreciation will, I believe, serve to illustrate.

Modern science will attempt to explain such imperfections away by leaning on the theory that, in the process of continuous regeneration of cells of the body, in following the true genetic formula passed down from antecedents, errors are made. Almost certainly correct, but to date no one has answered the question, why?

For the moment then, reverting back to my dear, old gran. 'What if she knew more than she was telling, or indeed, more than she understood? Just where, did all those so-called 'housewives' tales' originate, anyway?'

Now let us consider the possibility that apart from, as aforementioned, the obvious, some changes in facial appearance are the direct result of socially-less-acceptable, self-indulgent thoughts and actions. Those, that because others may judge them unworthy of us, are best kept secret. Yes, if you will, the lengthening of ear-lobes, the result of telling lies.

But then, most of us consider ourselves relatively honest. After all, it was in our upbringing – with for the unworthy, the ultimate penalty of shame. And so in keeping things to oneself – and thus electing conscience alone as judge and jury – what is to prevent the subconscious doling out punishment on the body. Seemingly this is the ideal way of preventing the overburdening of conscience as, day on day, yet more indiscretions of one sort or another are privately tucked away in the subconscious.

But, I hear you protest, just because someone is ugly, surely does not condemn them as a liar and a cheat? Certainly not, is the response, for such features may well have been ordained at birth.

No, it is not the intention here to create a yard-stick with which to judge others. Ever changing, more it is one by which we are reminded of our own ill-doing, one which perhaps may help us develop an attitude towards our fellow beings less 'holier-than-thou'.

At which point, to illustrate the point further, it seems appropriate to introduce two of the personalities involved in this research. Like my friend Andy, who would have been quite happy for his real name to have been used here. Then there is my own contribution to evidence, now by light of day growing visibly.

However, the following example might well be said to be common in most, sexually-active individuals. For, the existence of the phenomenon is well known – though few would openly confess to it – as is obvious.

So to which terrible sin do Andy and I confess? Well again perhaps there is need of a preamble; which in itself, hopefully, will answer the cries of innocence I know will be forthcoming at my assertion. For at this stage, my guess is that the majority of readers will be sitting astride a 'high-horse', in no way prepared to accept any hidden fault in their legitimate love-making. But, my friends, be ready for bruises to come – mostly to the opposite side of the anatomy currently under review.

It is fact that the behaviour about to be described is less likely in the young, particularly in today's laissez-faire world, where promiscuity is less frowned on, resulting in much freer, sexual activity between the sexes. The consequence is, there is less likelihood of fantasising during the act itself.

Such underhand behaviour, I would suggest, is far more likely to exist within older, more permanent, long-term relationships. For here, familiarity, as they say, breeds contempt and with the intent during the act itself of adding spice to individual enjoyment, often the face and more attractive figure of some unattainable, but fancied, partner enters the sexual daydreams of at least one of a regular pair of lovers. Unfaithful thoughts which go, of course, unrevealed, later stored in the subconscious to await another occasion of titillation - thereafter in turn, eventually to await the verdict of and consequential punishment by conscience to the body. Such, is just one of our sins. For neither Andy or myself is there need of denial. For on our separate paths through life, to our shame we have been guilty of such sins many times. So, given earlier assertions, what have been the consequences, the penalties exercised by conscience? Well, as he readily accepts, for the unfortunate Andy the main result has been the development of unsightly pitted skin and the growth of more than a few, ugly warts.

Conscience for me, however, for this particular transgression has exacted a more mischievous punishment, seemingly attempting to ensure for itself a regular, lifetime occupation.

In this regard, instead of being in deterioration, my appearance has gradually improved. For day by day, I become more handsome and thus more attractive to the opposite gender; and so, one would think, more likely to continue in my sinning.

However, there is irony in all of this, as in other ways the effect has been visibly cruel. For it is not for nothing that I have been allotted the nickname Dumbo – the hard-hearted calling from enemies and so-called friends alike. And so, my 'innocent' friend, think on – and yourself, be sure to keep a regular eye on the mirror.

VIII
SHADOWY PASSAGE

For many a year it was a forgotten memory. But revived by today's experience, suddenly it was returned to mind. As I remember, we were in the process of leaving the dark confines of the entry at the side of the house. It was a warm, sunny day and the street at the top of the entry was as brightly sunlit as ever I had seen it. Martin, my eighteen-month-old son, was raring to go and for once had escaped the immediate attention of his mother and myself.

Excitedly rushing ahead, the young mite reached the end of the dark tunnel and stepped out onto the sun-beaten flags of the street pavement beyond. There, of a sudden he was screaming, obsessed, so it seemed, by his feet. As though vainly attempting to avoid the scorching heat of a bed of red-hot coals, turning firstly this way then that he danced about on tip-toes, eventually taking flight, his short, stubby legs pumping up and down, carrying him away as fast as they were able.

For the moment thrown into panic and confusion, his parents were unable to fathom the tot's problem. However, parental instinct happily saved the day as we set off in pursuit of the terrified child. Finally catching up with him and in unison taking hold of his flailing arms, he was lifted from his feet into the comfort of his mother's arms, where eventually, through the whimpering the cause of his distress was voiced.

One year and a half he may have been, but suddenly, it seemed, Martin had discovered his shadow, and that 'the nasty thing' followed him everywhere – for 'an oh so little lad', a very frightening experience indeed.

Then, just as importantly recalled were later days, when Martin's younger sister, Celeste, 'invented' Gunby, a small boy – so we understood – of her imagination. Gunby became Celeste's constant friend and companion, for many months enjoying her protection and of course all her activities.

With the sympathetic acceptance of all, the phantom was soon to become a permanent member of the family, with, as proof of existence, a permanent place at the table. Here he must be lavished with attention, together with his sponsor enjoying, as dictated by Celeste, ample portions of 'their' favourite food and drink. And so it continued, until one fine day in her life, inexplicably Celeste abandoned her childhood friend.

The common denominator of the two recollections as above recounted – the basis of this story – is the phenomenon known as shadow. For, as a now much older and more rational Martin often teasingly remarked, in the sun Gunby had no shadow. And, of course, with no visible substance to his sister's playmate, certainly there was never any possibility of finding one.

However, although obvious to all, no one, not even Martin, dare argue the point with Celeste, she, quite rationally declaring that other than when the sun was shining or in lamplight, neither had anyone else a shadow. Therefore, as it was for everyone else in those conditions, so it was for Gunby, but for him it was the same in all situations. In her simple mind, her friend had not yet learned how to cast his shadow.

As in later years Martin himself remarked: "How do you argue against that?"

And so it is that, if the reader will excuse a pun and a simile, a shadow is cast across this story. For, with an ambulance recently arrived at the scene of the crash, provided by paramedics, I lie here dazed on a litter. Filling my eyes, a picture of dazzling lights then of dark shapes, alternately twisting first this way then that, at times gathering speed, then slowing to a halt. In the more stable moments, vision is as if through a child's toy kaleidoscope, a spinning jigsaw with pieces of consequence constantly to-ing and fro-ing, as though lost, searching for their place. That I am the victim of concussion enters the confusion of my mind. Strangely, however, remembering seems not to be a problem. After all, everything recorded this far has been unimpeded. In fact, apart from, as described, the strange effects on vision, everything else seems fine. Just lucky, I suppose. Not many would survive a high-speed crash and at that, terrifyingly head-on.

As I recall, with nowhere to go and having duly slammed on the brakes, I had been forced to watch on helplessly, as frighteningly the blinding headlamps of a great, 'mechanical monster' bore down on me.

For the driver of the lorry, it happened just as the central barrier ended, denoting the immediate change from dual to single carriageway. Travelling in the opposite direction towards me, poor judgement on his part left his sixty-foot, articulated lorry only part way through a reckless, overtaking manoeuvre. As he ploughed head-on into my small, defenceless car, I was praying for a miracle.

Now, for my suffering eyes, here is another blinding shaft of light to contend with. Does no one realise the discomfort I am suffering with my sight? But no, everyone seems to be occupied elsewhere and for the first time I wonder how others fared in the crash.

'The lorry driver, had he survived? If so, how badly was he hurt? And the vehicle he had been overtaking, the driver and possible passengers, what had become of them? I must think less of my own situation. At least I am alive and seemingly will survive.'

Now the source of the ever-increasing light becomes apparent. In all its brilliance, behold the rising sun. Gratefully, I am witnessing another dawn and from the looks of it, another beautiful, English summer's day is in prospect. Despite the dazzling discomfort, spirits are raised by the thought.

But now the picture is clearing and from my limited, physical position, as I am, laid out on the stretcher, I begin to see more of that around me. Dashing here, dashing there, a flurry of bodies are about their business of caring – an attribute of humanity, evidence of which never fails to move me.

But something is wrong; something strangely amiss. With all that had gone before and its effect on eyesight, at first it failed to register. Suddenly lost is the body-warming sensation of elation. Instead, suddenly I feel numb, a growing lump bringing a painful ache to the pit of the stomach.

In horror, the reason becomes terrifyingly clear. Born of panic, I try to voice my fears but, for the moment denied control of bodily functions, involuntarily the attempt manifests itself only as a blood-curdling scream, rendering the words unintelligible.

Frustrated time after time, finally I win the battle and in despairing hope of an answer, sound forth with 'What happened to the shadows? Please, please won't somebody answer me? For God's sake, where are the shadows?'

IX
CHARITABLE ACT

Although at the time I would not have known the difference, it might be said that it was not as exciting then as it has become since. For during the Second World War, in shopping for clothes or shoes it wasn't exactly brand-new my mother had in mind for me or indeed anyone else in the family. For during those austere days of government rationing, a common sight in the towns and cities of the war-torn islands of Great Britain were the popular, clothing swop-shops.

And as busy as the stores of today are at sale time, these essential exchange marts always were more so, catering as they did at a fraction of the cost of new for all and sundry, whatever sex, shape, size or age.

They were, of course, particularly ideal for children. For as they became older and outgrew their earlier size of clothing, so then, for a small charge, these would be passed on to those of appropriate stature; the donors themselves benefiting from the availability of a choice of passed-down clothing of their own, now larger fitting.

And so we progressed through childhood perhaps more so than today's younger generations, more appreciative of buying new, particularly so in such an affluent society. But then I hear the question, why the need for, so similar to the old swop-shops, the plethora of charity shops currently springing up on our high streets? And why, strangely, is the market for these outlets probably mostly comprised of a goodly age those once upon a time compelled to use the old swop-shops?

Not so strange, of course, is the answer. No longer related to lack of supply of goods, now such patronage is dictated by level of income, in particular lack of it. And so it will surprise no one to learn that, as an elderly widower, in common with many of the generation forced to survive on a government pension, much time is given to touring these charitable institutions searching out bargains. But it was within this activity that I was to discover what I believe to be a strange act of charity, one that was to have an effect on my life beyond belief. For, although I believe in always looking smart, lately, as the reader will understand, clothing myself has not been a top priority. The consequence being that, as I say, driven into making a choice from the racks of charity shops, even so, only items within a limited budget find their way into my sparsely-filled wardrobe.

It was, therefore, of great surprise both to myself and close friends, when I turned up for the A.G.M of the local golf club, garbed sprucely in a gentleman's suit which undoubtedly had set back its original owner several hundred pounds. A few years old it may have been, but nevertheless earning more than the occasional glance from the snob fraternity, it was instantly recognised as of 'Savile Row'. However, needless to relate, its cost to me had been but a small fraction of its original price – a bargain indeed.

Later, driving home, I was perhaps not quite so attentive to the task at the wheel as I might have been. Playing a prominent role in the ladies' golf section, my mind was on Millicent Ford. Earlier, at the meeting, I had been aware of occasional, meaningful looks from her direction.

No, it was not imagination. Always attractively dressed, the handsome Mrs Ford was a widow: her husband, as I had been led to believe, having passed away in recent times. As it was for me with most of the lady members, prior contact with Millicent Ford had been limited to an introduction at a club dance some years earlier and thereafter to polite exchanges of greeting on the course and around the clubhouse. Not that I did not find her attractive, but tonight's obvious interest was unprecedented and somewhat of a shock. Hence, as now I drove down a poorly lit back-street, with, in the way of a metronome, the car's wipers uncompromisingly sweeping aside the blurring effect of a light curtain of drizzle, lack of due care and attention was to involve me in an accident; one that may have been even more serious, except for my own, unusual behaviour.

No doubt in its slippery nature the wet surface of the road contributed greatly to the unfortunate event. But, ironically, it also played its part in the prevention of a possible fatality, due in part to its mirroring quality. For as the driver of the car in front was suddenly confronted by an unlit bicycle directly in his path and viciously stamped on the brake, momentarily torn from my self-indulgent musing I was dazzled by the reflection of the bright-red of his brake-lights, itself, to a small degree delaying my own braking reaction.

The resulting collision between the two cars was happily minimal. However, the erring, young cyclist was tossed into the gutter, where puddles of rain were gathering, in part strangely coloured with a young man's blood.

In a stunned state of shock, the driver of the leading car seemed unable to act, remaining at the steering wheel motionless. But for me, dreamlike, it was as though I was someone else, someone who quickly dismounted and, rapidly in crouched position down on his knees - unusually with no care of the soiling of trousers - quickly administered medical attention to the injured lad. Then, with the prime patient relatively comfortable, my alter ego went to the aid of the other driver, checking first for physical damage, then, satisfied all was well, helping him to recover his wits.

As later eventually I arrived home, having halted the car, retaining a firm grip on the steering wheel I too remained glued to the seat. As if in a trance, staring down the beams of the headlamps, my mind was full of the strange events of the evening. Until this very moment failing to register discomfort, if it had not been for the pain of a sprained wrist, all might have been a dream.

Then there was the earlier situation of Millicent Ford's seeming attraction towards me. 'Just what, was going on there?' Whatever it was, if and until she broached the subject, I determined to say nothing. And at the accident, 'just where did I find the knowledge and resourcefulness to do what I did?' As later in my bed I fell asleep, two extremely puzzling questions remained unanswered.

Of superior weave and tailoring quality, fortunately my new trousers were easily dry-cleaned and on their next airing were as good as new. As it happened, dress was formal for Sunday lunch at the golf club, where, since the A.G.M., I had to admit I had been making myself more available; half in hope, I suppose, that Millicent Ford would be there - although, I really had no idea why. Nevertheless it was yet another opportunity to show off my 'new' suit.

However, in retrospect, in this respect I suppose there was a vague resemblance to behaviour of my youth, when, smitten by some young female or other, dressed to the 'nines' I was to be found aimlessly hanging about her known haunts, willing an accidental meeting. But now beyond such nonsense, nothing would have persuaded me to admit to such immature conduct; although, as I say, Millicent was not without her charms.

And purely by coincidence of course, there, on this particular Sunday I bumped into her, as it happened in the company of a married couple, also friends of mine, so I took the opportunity to say hello before seeking out my own, allotted table. Discovering that I was on my own, of course they would have it no other way. I was to join them and found myself sitting directly opposite my quarry, her smile, of welcome I presumed, adding to the pleasurable intrigue of the moment.

But apart from the usual golfing chatter and day-to-day small talk, as might be expected in company nothing of Millicent's seeming interest in me on the night of the A.G.M. emerged. And so the meal progressed and with each mouthful, conversation was duly diminished.

Then suddenly disturbing the tranquility of the occasion, all about was mayhem, with waiting staff rushing here, there and everywhere and on the other side of the room diners inexplicably on their feet. Then came the cry of a single voice: "Is there a doctor here?"

Before I realised what was happening, I was on my feet offering assistance. As I reached his side... "this gentleman has collapsed" was all the restaurant manager was allowed before being rudely brushed aside, the would-be medic hastily dropping to his haunches to begin resuscitation.

If friends and fellow golfers were surprised at the whole performance, imagine my own, that of someone with not one iota of medical knowledge or training. Even more, picture the disbelief as, with a cough and a splutter, colour returning to his face, eventually the patient's breathing was resumed.

As it happened, the survivor himself was in medicine and later, after being made aware of the sum total of my own expertise in the science, namely nil, confessed total bewilderment at the whole affair. Apparently, he being allergic to shellfish, he had inadvertently consumed, hidden in a salad dressing, a small portion of shrimp.

The outcome had been a swelling of the tongue and throat, to the point of arrested respiration. With the use of a sharp knife and a plastic drinking straw, the action of performing a crude tracheotomy, so it seemed, saved his life. I was a hero. And no more so than to Millicent, who rushed to my side and throwing her arms around my embarrassed neck, kissed me fully on the lips; her surprising action supposedly born of relief and admiration.

The consequence was that later I was given the privilege of driving Millicent home, when, perhaps needless to report, talk between us was much freer than otherwise might have been. And how pleased I would be for that. For, in her sensitive handling of the facts she was about to impart to me, she was faultless. With anyone else I might have been embarrassed beyond experience, but she saved me that with her understanding and kindness. Otherwise galling and explaining Millicent's earlier, unusual interest in me, the first fact imparted was that as part of a complete wardrobe donated to the charity shop concerned, my new suit had been that of her husband.

But added to this was a fact which perhaps explains some of the mystery surrounding my doctoring experiences of late – although, in accepting the supposition, there is a need for belief in matters above and beyond the norm. For, until now unknown to myself, Millicent Ford's late husband had been an accomplished surgeon.

Could it be, that in the package of personal belongings bequeathed to charity, there had been included an extra, special gift?

X
CATNAP

Following the initial shock of physical removal from the comfortable existence afforded by her womb then, testing unlearned lungs with the first few breaths of warm, moist air, came the pleasure of meeting my mother.

At first this was to be found in her bodily warmth, instinctively creating a bond between us. Then, the object of a strong maternal instinct for hygiene, there was the sensation to my being of a rasping tongue as, ignoring my efforts to avoid the cleaning of certain, sensitive areas, determinedly yet with great tenderness she dutifully took to the task of grooming my soft but untidy coat. And so it was that, eyes still unopen, I and my siblings – four sisters and the runt of the litter, a much smaller brother – made our way into the world.

That was almost a year ago and with my mother, the mild-tempered 'Tessy', now sadly passed on and the remainder of her final litter happily finding homes elsewhere, today now answering to the name of 'Toby' I find myself the sole, four-legged member of the Osborne family, the kindly tall-people at number 48.

The name given to the busy main road on which **our** house stands – for without doubt I am treated as one of the family – is Woodside Avenue, truly an avenue boasting many glorious gardens, none more so than our own. But directly opposite, across the frightening, traffic-plagued road, is the neglected garden of a long-empty house. Indeed, as learned from recent, family conversations, since the former owners departed, nearly twelve months have passed.

In fact, as I remember, the benchmark used was, 'almost the same time as 'Tessy' gave birth to her six little ones, nearly a year ago.' An event, of course, which included myself.

Thus, the garden concerned, was – the opinion of all – an overgrown jungle. Conversely, because it was cultured and well-cared for, that at number 48 took second place in my choice of playground; the wasteland of long, unkempt grasses over the road much preferred.

But, as previously explained, in travelling from A to B and back again, terrifyingly there is a need to cross the busy road – for this young tom, strangely at the heart of many a blood-chilling nightmare. Nevertheless, with fears, if not exactly conquered, put to positive employment in exercising extreme caution, the journey is negotiated safely every day of the week – in early morning there and in late afternoon, again home.

Once there, with routine patrols – each day initially marking the bounds – 'the young master' of this jungle paradise ensures incursion by strangers goes not without warning. Then, in the event, alarmed by senses on high alert, with stilled body pressed low to the ground, a search is conducted beyond the familiar, seeking the reason for upset.

But, offensive or otherwise, rarely is there need for action. With all-over ginger, glossy coat, most times of alert it is only my all-time, number one friend – for obvious reasons dubbed by his owners, 'Carrot'. At such times, 'Carrot's performance is purposeful, he deliberately playing the part in battle manoeuvres. But never once has the ensuing encounter developed into anything other than harmless play.

But, vital to the defence of 'the realm' is the development and honing of skills in self-camouflage. Then also, the practising of the essential element of surprise, springing from cover without warning – most times, in itself enough to effect the hasty departure of an intruder.

However, real or imaginary, given the opportunity, a neutral observer would be hard put to detect the difference. Such is the intensity and realism of these formal manoeuvres.

Such activities, however, more likely are effected on unsuspecting friends, those perhaps not quite so aware as the ever faithful 'Carrot', who, though himself less concerned about territorial rights, helpfully recognises his best friend's need for combat readiness and is happy to provide in the matter, a sheathed claw or two.

At the time of this story the garden was enjoying the favours of high summer, the undergrowth providing many shady places where, after a perhaps stolen meal or an energetic chase, following a period of necessary grooming a busy boss-cat might take advantage of the opportunity to curl up, eventually to fall asleep.

On the day in question, as was so the day immediately prior, 'Carrot' was missing – for him, not unusual. Obviously he had found more important activities elsewhere. So for myself, confident of no interruptions from that direction, in mid-afternoon the order of the day was a refreshing nap.

Time on and again awake, with no obvious reason to abandon routine, the task of essential grooming was entered upon. In so doing it is of course necessary to twist neck and head around, tucking the latter under the body, allowing to the tongue easy access to soft, under-fur in hide-away places – as any self-respecting guard will attest, a time of least awareness.

On this occasion the habit carelessly allowed the approach of an interloper unobserved. Initial warning came via a friendly greeting from, as I assumed, a passing tall-person outside the garden.

"Well, hello there. Making ourselves handsome, are we?" Such was the surprise, it startled me out of my ablutions, fast returning me to a state of readiness; though, no one could be sure whether for attack or retreat.

But surprise rapidly changed to shock, in sudden realisation that I was in the close company of one of my own kind – as it happened, an extremely attractive female.

Surprise, shock and now total astonishment – for that is how matters developed. For, imagine the uneasiness of a young, innocent tomcat when, denying the earlier assumption of a voice of a passer-by, in perfect mimicry of a tall-person, my uninvited companion exclaimed: "Sorry! Obviously I've surprised you. I hope you'll forgive me."

There could be no greater truth. It was the greatest surprise to a young life one could imagine. So much so that, for the moment, in total awe of the situation, with jaw dropped, mouth agape, I was rendered incapable of answer.

Although with her long, smoke-grey skirt, beautiful eyes and cheeky turn-up of nose the most beautiful cat in the world, that she had penetrated my defences undetected, was disturbing. But more so, were her words and voice. Inexplicably, these were of the tall-people.

As is well recorded, feline interaction is usually achieved vocally, by mewing, purring, growling and the like. Then by the issuing of scent, communication is achieved through sense of smell. And movement also takes its part, with for example, indicating anger, the switching of the tail back and forth.

But, until this moment perhaps escaping the reader's notice, is my own strange ability to understand the spoken word; a phenomenon which, one can be assured, is indeed unusual. In evidence it is offered that, although in the early days not apparent, to my certain knowledge, apart from the odd word, not my mother, not 'Carrot' nor any other cat of my acquaintance has ever mastered the art. So what was now being witnessed was frighteningly without precedent.

But refusing the use of one superlative for another, in describing my own state of mind and body, bemusing me more was my own eventual response – surprisingly issued in the same medium. Although involuntarily so, this was my first attempt at mimicking the conversation of the tall-people, in answer hesitantly stammering: "Er, sorry. No, er, everything's fine. But, I don't understand. Just how, are you, er sorry, we, able to talk together like this?"

Then, forced to clear my aching throat, the resulting, unintended growl was mistaken for aggression. At which, an alarmed female, the fine hairs of her coat, in fear standing on end, instinctively retreated, back arched.

"Look, I'm sorry," I told her hurriedly, again stammering. "I didn't mean to startle you." Confounding reason, the strange words were formulated somewhere deep inside.

Understandably the result was not immediate. However, with words and sentences somehow carefully chosen to calm the situation, very soon we were friends, my new acquaintance eventually offering an apology of her own.

"Look, I'm sorry too," she proffered. "After all, this is all my fault. It must have been a terrible shock for you when you first heard me talking this way. You see, ever since I discovered the ability, in belief of the existence of others I have been searching high and low for someone the same. But no one has ever responded, until now. You're the very first. So you can see this is just as surprising for me. Nevertheless, I am sorry to alarm you so. Please, won't you forgive me?"

At this point, with no experience in the matter, interpretation of her now more relaxed, bodily pose was purely instinctive. Most certainly she was female and, to this young tomcat, provocatively so – and perhaps more importantly, I felt I could trust her. And so, following my acceptance of her supplication, we grew closer, barriers falling one by one, as over the time of daylight remaining to us, we learned more of each other.

Apparently, shortly after her birth, the family she had been born to had moved abroad, taking her with them. But some four or five months later, having decided to return home here to Woodside Avenue, their pet was subjected to compulsory quarantine. It had been six months of misery, living away from the love of her tall-people family. They, she was told, were distraught at the thought of her loneliness. But with her recent release, happily they were now reunited, all living together again next door, where she was born.

And so, in our chat, raised was the subject of age, and added to our common linguistic ability, yet more coincidence. For now we learned that, although born on opposite sides of the road, of the same year, strangely we shared the same birth-date, we both now being almost one-year-old.

But if she was to be believed, the most startling revelation was, the claimed recollection of a previous life. And at that, as one of the tall-people, to which, for me, the strange fact of her linguistic expertise added a bizarre truth. But in now recounting this tale, judgement surely must lie with others.

With introductions made earlier, names had little use or meaning until now. But at this point, 'Candice' – for that was her given name – chose to confess that the name 'Toby' was well known to her, but not in a cat.

For as she then further revealed, the names of the married tall-people couple previously occupying the house directly behind us, had been 'Candice'and 'Toby', coincidence or not, the same as our own. Then, as only one who was there might do, she disclosed all she knew of the young couple's life together, with every fact divulged the story becoming more and more convincing.

But it was when finally she gave her explanation for the pair's hurried departure from the scene, that the tensing of muscles along the line of my spine, lifting its thick covering of hairs, brush-like, gave me away. Understandably I was completely disconcerted. For within her description of events, she and 'Candice' of the tall-people, were one in the same being – this now, for her, being the afterlife.

'Could this be real? Was I not dreaming?' But no, feigning an irritation to the skin, I took a moment to scratch myself, and certainly this was reality, a rogue claw taking quite a toll on the area chosen for attention. 'But in taking account of her assertion, why was she choosing to tell, of all people, me? And why, surprisingly, was I feeling so involved?'

The answer, she told me, lay in all that she now knew, with the long-missing piece of a mind-blowing jigsaw provided by her latest acquaintance, myself – coincidence or not, going by the name of 'Toby'. For, if there was any acceptable explanation to this tale of coincidences, certainly it seemed it was the one she now proffered.

Perhaps accounting for all that she claimed as fact – and thus far unmentioned in our frank and open discussion, one other indisputable fact – almost one year ago to the day, coincident with our common birthday, whilst returning home from holiday, 'Candice' and 'Toby' were involved in a dreadful car crash, with both tragically killed.

Given then, acceptance of the premise of my being the re-incarnation of 'Toby', 'Candice's husband, is there any wonder the traffic on the road between here and home, holds for me such terror – an incontrovertible fact. And given the obvious, growing attraction between myself and this fairest of females –

and hopefully, a happy hereafter together – surely then, there can be no harm in the belief of an afterlife? Or can there?

XI
WISH YOU WERE HERE

"Even though it was the most sultry summer either of us had ever experienced, 'Diana' was adamant; she wanted a holiday abroad, and believe it or not, in the sun. I can't say I was totally against it, so I agreed to visit a travel agent in the town with her where, hopefully in booking last minute, we might benefit from a saving. The thing was, Chief Inspector, we were prepared to fly at short notice, taking a chance on the type of accommodation available; self-catering if necessary. However, 'Diana' was adamant about her choice of destination; yet again it was to be 'Corfu', her all-time favourite resort.

"So, you might ask, how did we come to find ourselves in '**Crete**'? Well, as it happened, our first choice had been over-fancied with no bargains left on offer; just as well perhaps, since the beaches would no doubt have been overcrowded.

Anyway, Chief Inspector, to return to your question, it was as we settled into our accommodation that we first encountered the 'Crofts'. As it happened, they were our next-door neighbours and hearing us move in, they called on us to introduce themselves.

First impressions...? Well, certainly not slow in coming forward and of course, very friendly. All in all a thoroughly nice pair although they did seem a bit of an odd couple.

Literally dripping with heavy gold chains and rings, 'Bill Croft', appeared particularly well-heeled for, as it turned out, a self-employed, one-man, self-employed builder and decorator.

But he was nondescript compared to his wife who, apart from the customary engagement ring and wedding band, strangely went totally without jewellery — and with little need: 'Lauren Croft' simply oozed sex appeal, and from the very first flutter of those long, black eyelashes in my direction - despite the constant presence of my wife - appeared to be offering something more than platonic friendship; although, 'Bill' too took little notice of this supposed flirting.

"Nevertheless, from the start the girls got on like a house on fire, my wife seemingly oblivious to any possibility of her new friend's advances towards me. Or maybe it was all in my imagination; for it has to be said that there was little else to suggest any waywardness in her.

"Anyway, Chief Inspector, as things progressed, it became clear that our neighbours, who had arrived a week earlier, were no str'angers to the island and discovering this to be our first visit, insisted on showing us around.

And so we became constant companions, rarely venturing out one pair without the other. However, nearly always to be found together engrossed in girl talk, more it was 'Diana' and 'Lauren' who became the closest. But then again, although of different worlds at home, 'Bill' and I found we had enough in common simply as married men of the world to form a bond.

"Evening entertainment was non-stop for all of us as a group: tavernas, hotel bars, barbeques, discotheques, shows and the like. Daytime would find the girls together, sunning themselves on the beach or shopping, whilst 'Bill' and I who preferred sightseeing, more often than not hired a car between us, taking it in turns at the wheel, driving up into the mountains in search of peace and tranquillity. However, as likely as not, most days would end with a quiet drink or two in hand enjoying the company of locals. Probably not much different to home, I suppose.

"Then all too soon the 'Crofts' holiday was over and given the forty odd miles between us at home, so too, we supposed, would be our friendship. However, as we saw them off at the airport, typically tearful the girls promised to visit each other sometime in the near future.

And that, Chief Inspector, is the last we saw or heard of them; this holiday being our first and only encounter with the 'Crofts'. Before that, we had never met; nor have we seen or been in touch with either of them since. Indeed, it was only when we tried the phone number they gave us to reach them here in Britain, we realised something might be wrong. For as you now know, Inspector, that phone number happened to be that of your own police station with the only 'Croft' at that number being young Sergeant 'Croft', who, surprisingly turns out to be their son. Crikey though, they must have had him early on in life; neither of them hardly seemed old enough to have a son that age; but then, maybe they're older than they looked.

And now you tell us they're both missing; I can't tell you how shocked we are. You learn of such things through the media of course, but really, it's not the sort of thing you expect to come up against yourself, is it? I'm only sorry we can't be of more help. It really is a mystery, isn't it?"

Deciding there was no need of response, instead, the investigating officer recorded his satisfaction with matters, declaring: "Well, Mr Gee thank you for such a full account of events. Mostly the details agree with those you gave us at your first interview and those previously by your wife. At this time there are no further questions but, can I ask that if in the near future you plan to spend any significant length of time away from home please be good enough to notify us beforehand."

As the straight-faced chief inspector ended, he and the accompanying detective sergeant made their apologies and rose to their feet, anxious to beat the evening traffic rush-hour out of town and return to the centre of operations in the 'Crofts' hometown.

"Well, what a way to end a holiday," 'Diana' declared when the two unexpected visitors had gone. Then, expressing obvious relief, through pursed lips in a near whistle she made a show of expelling the remaining breath in her body before continuing: "Who would have believed it? Home not a week and a visit from the police. It's unreal – like a bad dream.

And what about the photos? Of those taken solely of the 'Crofts', none have come out; and of those with all of us together, we're both there but 'Laura' and 'Bill's images are both blanked out. What's that all about? It's the weirdest thing ever, don't you think?"

"So, O'Brien, what did you make of the Gees?" 'Derek Boulten' asked of his subordinate, the detective sergeant now relegated to a driving job behind the wheel of an unmarked, black 'Ford Orion'.

"Can't say there was anything about either of them that suggested they were telling porkies," he replied, his attention at the wheel unwavering. "Both seemed genuinely shocked by the news. It's doubtful they **were** hiding anything. However, if they were, they both put on a damned good act. But in that we've interviewed both of them separately, on two separate occasions, from their individual behaviours my sixth sense tells me not."

"Personally, I think you're right," the older, more experienced officer agreed. "But especially at this early stage of the investigation, we both know not to draw conclusions, **don't we**, Sergeant?"

"That we do, sir," concurred the Anglo-Irishman, delivering his words in the usual, tell-tale Irish brogue, "that we do."

"Best not to reveal the full story too, don't you think? Although, when the Press get hold of this, as no doubt they will, everyone will know soon enough – and then all and sundry will be making their own assumptions.

After all, that the Crofts disappeared ten years ago then mysteriously reappeared on holiday in the company of the Gees 3 weeks ago is totally beyond belief."

Constantly frustrated by the paparazzi's uncontrolled involvement and oft-times destructive interference, with eyes lifted to the heavens, an expression of disgusted resignation invaded the face of the senior man, this then finalising the conversation, both men falling into deep, puzzled silence.

But running through the senior officer's head, something at the heart of the mystery totally defying explanation was, that telephone number: that of his own police station, the one rung by the 'Gees', supposedly given to them by the 'Crofts'. And how could it be that the Crofts' son was stationed there. Given that for whatever reason, the Crofts had planned all this and had indeed disappeared ten years ago when their son was still at school, how then could they possibly know he would join the police force and indeed be stationed in his home town; and on top of that, know the telephone number of that station? After all, from the interview with Sergeant 'Croft' himself, it was quite obvious he was very upset and totally bemused by the situation.

Added to this, of course, is the negative result of our enquiries with the airlines in and out of 'Crete' in recent weeks: neither of the 'Crofts' were registered on any passenger list, nor at any of the airport check-in desks concerned, nor indeed with any of the immigration control authorities. Thorough checks at the 'Gees' hotel in 'Crete', local tourist offices and the island's local police proffered similar, negative results.

As far as they were concerned, the 'Crofts' did not exist.

Then there are the enquiries made into possible fraud; those made on national and international criminal computer bases, and of course those with the insurance companies. Indeed, in the latter case, with no bodies to confirm one way or the other, death was not proven so no great sums of money, or indeed any at all, had been paid out against the claim made by the 'Crofts' estates, which to this day remain 'not settled'.

Irrationally, for the Inspector, more and more the possibility that this might just be an effort to contact their son from the 'other side' worried him.

So too he worried for the 'Gees', for in as much as he knew they were anxious for their friends' being, he was pretty sure that given all the circumstances they would perhaps prefer not to receive any correspondence from the Crofts: especially if it expressed the overused greeting, 'Wish you were here'.